ONION TEARS

ONION TEARS

DIANA KIDD

illustrated by L U C Y M O N T G O M E R Y

ORCHARD BOOKS
New York

Orchard Books
A division of Franklin Watts, Inc.
387 Park Avenue South
New York, NY 10016

Manufactured in the United States of America. Book design by Jean Krulis.

10 9 8 7 6 5 4 3 2 1

The text of this book is set in 13 point Goudy Old Style. The illustrations are graphite drawings.

Library of Congress Cataloging-in-Publication Data
Kidd, Diana. Onion tears / Diana Kidd. — 1st American ed. p. cm.
Summary: A little Vietnamese girl tries to come to terms with her grief over the loss of her family and her new life with the Australian family with whom she lives. ISBN 0-531-05870-0. ISBN 0-531-08470-1 (lib. bdg.) [1. Vietnamese—Australia—Fiction. 2. Grief—Fiction. 3. Foster home care—Fiction.] I. Title. PZ7.K52950n 1991
[Fic]—dc20 90-43011

For Valerie Falk
and Gnocchi

ACKNOWLEDGMENTS

The author acknowledges the use of excerpts and information from *Why Must We Go?—Descriptions of Journeys to Australia from South-east Asia by South-east Asian Students of Richmond Girls' High School* (published by Richmond Girls' High School, Richmond, Victoria, Australia, 1981. Compiled and edited by Valerie R. Falk, B.A. Dip.Ed.) and in particular, stories by Nga Ho, Ngoc Huong, Hue Kim Chau, Hao Ngoc La, Uyen and Hue Tran.

The excerpt "Life is like a fleet-footed horse passing by a crevice" was taken from "My Journey" by Ngoc Huong.

Thanks to the following people for their help:
Phan thi Anh Tuyet, Nguyen Quoc Huy, Phan Sac Phan, Anna Soo, Valerie Falk, Simon Kidd, Liz Air.

Special thanks to Cathie Tasker for her help and support throughout the joys and dramas of computerizing this book.

ONION TEARS

Auntie gets really mad at me when I leave my room in a mess.

"Nam-Huong!" she shouts. "Tidy up your room before Mr. and Mrs. Ngoc come to visit. It looks like wild monkeys live in there."

Auntie's funny when she's cross. She stamps her feet and yells at Chu Minh and me.

"Chu Minh—the soup tastes like a salt mine! Nam-Huong—those prawns will grow whiskers if you don't hurry up and finish peeling them!"

Sometimes, when she's finished shouting, Auntie makes a pot of jasmine tea. She puts a lace cloth on the table and gets out her best blue-and-white cups, and we all sit down and drink it together. And sometimes she gives us a chocolate from the big box that she keeps hidden under the counter.

Auntie's always very busy. She runs the restaurant all by herself. Lots of people come for dinner. Last night there were fifty, and Auntie was cross with Chu Minh because nearly everyone ordered *dim sims* and he hadn't made enough. (I saw him eat six of those dumplings when Auntie wasn't looking.)

He's always running out of things and making Auntie mad.

She's not my real auntie. I just call her that. She's looking after me until I find my mom and dad.

Every day after school I creep upstairs and lie on the floor and watch TV. But I can still hear Auntie downstairs in the restaurant banging saucepans and shouting at Chu Minh while he prepares the fish.

As soon as she finds out that I'm there she calls me to come and help. It makes my hand

tired chopping all those onions. I have to do it really fast.

I hate chopping smelly onions. My eyes sting and pour tears like monsoon rains.

Everyone at school keeps asking me what my name means.

"Does it mean princess?" Mary says.

"*Coconut!*" Tessa shouts.

"Butterfly!" "Dragon!" They all try and guess.

"I know," says Danny. "It means *dim sim*!"

But I just shake my head.

One day I'll tell them what it means.

My mom loved my name. She said it was very special.

There's a tree house at the back of our school. It's called Phantom House. All the boys climb up and play there. Mary and Tessa do, too.

But I've never been up there.

Sometimes I sit on the grass and watch, just like I did at home in our village when the boys climbed the palm trees for coconuts, and I remember my house and the fruit trees that grew on the other side of the river, and how we swam across and climbed up and picked the wild fruit. I gave some to my little sister, Lan, and she got a pain in her stomach.

But it's different living here with Auntie. She'd get mad if I climbed up a tree.

Today Mary said, "Want to play in Phantom House?"

I shook my head.

Then Danny sang a horrible song.

> *"Nam is dumb.*
> *She hasn't got a tongue."*

And after school Mary said, "Want to come up to the shops, Nam? I'll give you a ride."

I shook my head again.

"She's too scared," Danny yelled, and he did a wheelie on his bike.

"No, she's not. She's just shy."

"What's wrong with her anyway?" said

Tessa. "Why doesn't she talk? She doesn't even laugh when I tickle her. Why doesn't she? Why won't she be friends?"

I can never tell them why.

I can never tell them why I am like the wooden duck that Grandpa carved for me so long ago.

I liked doing things with my grandpa. Sometimes we walked together in the evening and watched the sun setting.

When we climbed the hill, Grandpa would puff a lot and fall over in the prickly grass. Then I'd pull the burrs from his hair and push him all the way up to the top.

He always brought his flute with him, the one he made from bamboo. I liked the tunes he played—they were the sounds of birds and the sea and the wind.

He played them over and over again until the sun disappeared behind the next hill.

After school today I wrote a letter to my best friend in all the world.

Dear little yellow canary,

Do you remember me?

It's so long since I saw you.

You are still my best friend. I like you better than all the hens, better than the buffalo, better than the snake that came to drink at our well, better than the baby pigs, and even better than the duck.

Do you remember the first day you came to live in our house? My grandpa found you in the long grass— you couldn't fly because you'd hurt your wing. So Grandpa made a cage for you out of bamboo and I fed you every evening with some rice on the end of my finger.

And one day you started to whistle—so beautifully. Then my mom and dad and Grandpa and Lan and my little brothers, Tri and Son and Tho, all came and stood around the cage listening to you.

Every time I washed the dishes you would sing and make me feel better while I was working. If I went outside to play I would say good-bye to you and you'd hop up and down as if you wanted to go with me, too.

8

And when I was feeling lonely I would sit and talk to you and tell you everything, just as if you were my best friend.

Dear little yellow canary, I have been here all the springtime and seen the trees smiling with pink blossoms. And now it's summer.

At home it will be hot and wet. Have the rains flooded our paddy field?

Have you seen my mom and dad?

I miss you.

You are my best friend in all the world.

I wonder where you are now.

Are you singing somewhere in a tree?

Nam-Huong

"Why don't you find a nice girl and get married?" Auntie says to Chu Minh every day. "Marry a nice girl and then she can help us here in the restaurant."

"I'm not getting married!" he groans, and cuts the rice paper all crooked and spills the fish sauce all over the place. And then he says, "Nam-Huong! Just look at those onions. They're like flying saucers! Can't you cut them

9

finer? And the carrots—they look like you've chopped them with an ax!"

Imagine anyone marrying Chu Minh! He's a champion at judo. If his wife didn't slice the onions thin enough, he'd pick her up with one hand and throw her out of the window.

Chu Minh is good at tricks, too. He can balance a wineglass on the end of his nose (when Auntie isn't looking). But his knife trick is the best. He can twirl a knife all by itself 'round and 'round his thumb.

"All the best cooks can do that," he says.

Chu Minh makes me smile inside.

Chu Minh and I have been chopping onions again—hundreds of them. And I've cried hundreds of tears, too.

Onion tears.

It's so easy to cry onion tears.

Why can't I cry real ones?

I wish I could cry real ones.

On Friday and Saturday nights I help Auntie

and Chu Minh in the restaurant. Sometimes I carry the plates in and clear the tables.

It's really hard carrying the soup so that it doesn't spill all over the place. Last night we had *pho* soup and I helped Chu Minh chop up the chicken and cook the noodles.

Later on, when I went up to my room, the smell of the soup crept up there with me.

I lay on my bed and closed my eyes and I saw my mom and my dad and Lan and Tri and Son and Tho and Grandpa—sitting around the table eating rice and soup. *Pho* soup was my dad's favorite.

"Your mother makes the best *pho* in the whole world," my dad always said.

I had *cha gio* for lunch today.

Danny sat next to me and poked his fingers in my lunch box and said, "What's that funny stuff?"

Our teacher wears earrings with big red parrots dangling from them. Her hair is long and frizzy.

Her name is long, too, so she told us just to call her Miss Lily.

Danny calls her Miss Lily-Longlegs.

When she gets cross with Danny, her voice screams around the ceiling and flies out the window like a mad wasp.

Danny says she lives in a spooky house at the end of Francis Street. He says it's haunted. "It's got thirteen ghosts," I heard him tell Mary. Tessa said she saw one staring through the window when she rode past Miss Lily's house the other day on the way to the beach.

And she said there's a palm tree in Miss Lily's garden. Danny says that at night it turns into a hairy witch.

One day I want to get some perfume like Miss Lily's. I saw a bottle of it on her desk today. It's got a picture of some yellow flowers on it—just like the flowers that grew in my uncle's garden.

Uncle had lots of palm trees in his garden, too—and there were mangoes and oranges and bananas.

My mom said Uncle was rich. I liked going to his house. He always gave us fresh fish—not the dried fish that we had at home. He gave us ice cream, too—lots of it. We were really lucky that our uncle had an ice-cream factory in the city.

In summertime when we visited him all the fruit was ripe. I liked the mangoes best. So did Lan. The juice dribbled all over her face and down her arms and in between her toes and all over the blue shirt that Mom had made her.

There were snakes with four legs in my uncle's garden. When one of them stared at Lan with its long tongue flicking in and out, she screamed and grabbed my skirt, and I had to save her from that awful creature.

There were ghosts in my uncle's garden, too—right at the end behind the banana tree with its long green leaves that swayed from side to side like old elephants.

"That's where the ghosts live," I'd tell Lan, and she'd scream and run inside.

When Lan grows up I'll take her to the end of my uncle's beautiful garden.

*　　*　　*

Some birds came to stay at our school today.

"The swallows are here again," Miss Lily said. "They have come south looking for summer."

She showed us their nest hidden under the eaves outside our classroom window.

Dear little swallows, I thought. Did you fly over my country? Did you see my mom and dad? Did you see my little yellow canary?

Danny wrote a poem today and he showed it to everyone.

> Rice and pork
> and funny black sauce.
>
> Whose lunch is it?
>
> Nam's lunch

Sometimes on Sundays, Auntie and I go to the park with Mr. and Mrs. Ngoc and their three children.

I like playing with them. We collect autumn

14

leaves and crunch them in our hands to make them crackle.

Then I help Auntie put up the folding table so that we can have our lunch.

But last Sunday I saw Tessa and everyone riding their bikes and playing soccer.

And I didn't like being Nam-Huong.

I wished I weren't Nam-Huong.

I want to be like Tessa and play soccer with the boys and climb trees and ride a bike with no hands—and I want to take sandwiches and cakes to school for lunch instead of all that stuff my auntie gives me.

When we got back from the park I wrote another letter to my best friend.

Dear little yellow canary,

Do you remember that night when the soldiers came? I was lying in the hammock and you were whistling so beautifully because I'd just given you some rice.

But my dad wasn't hungry that night. He didn't eat his rice or his soup. He kept getting up from the table and looking out of the window.

"Soldiers," he said to Mom. "They were seen near the village this morning."

It was while I was talking to you, little canary, that there was a loud banging on the door. I heard my mom and dad whispering, and then there was an awful silence as if the world had stopped.

Dear little yellow canary, you and I screamed and cried and hid in a corner when the soldiers pushed our door down and took my dad away.

Dear little yellow canary, have you seen my dad?

Have you seen my mom and Lan and Tri and Son and Tho?

I have written lots of letters to them—but they never answer.

16

My new auntie has written lots of letters, too.
Why don't they answer?
Dear little yellow canary, where are they?

Nam-Huong

Chu Minh likes collecting things. When he goes to the dump with trash from the restaurant, he always brings something back with him.

His room is full of all sorts of things that he's going to fix one day. There's a toaster and a vase and there are plates and lamps and a machine for chopping up things. He's got three televisions that he's pulled to bits and an old stroller that he left in the shed so that he could paint it for Mrs. Ngoc's new baby, but next door's cat had six kittens in it before he had time to fix it.

Sometimes when she tries to clean his room, Auntie gets mad and stamps her feet and yells.

"Chu Minh, I'm pleased for you to have a room in my house and I'm happy for you to live here. But I just want *you* in that room, not the entire dump as well. However can I clean it! How can I clean it?"

Then, when she has finished exploding, she puts her arm in his and says, "Don't worry, Chu Minh, I don't really mind—my home is your home—but please close your door when

Mr. and Mrs. Ngoc and my friends come to visit."

And then she says, "Come on now, let's all sit down and have some tea."

When I was getting out the cups and teapot Auntie put her arm around my shoulders and whispered, "Chu Minh has only had hunger and sadness all his life. And here there is everything. He can have the whole dump in his room if he likes."

Sometimes I really like Auntie.

Every day after school I rush to see if the postman has brought a letter for me.

But he never does.

I have written hundreds of letters to my mom.

Why doesn't she answer?

Today Mary said, "Want to play a game of hopscotch?"

But I just shook my head.

Last night I couldn't sleep, because someone

had a party in the restaurant and they made a lot of noise. So I wrote another letter.

Dear little duck as white as a cloud,

It's so long since I saw you. Do you still remember me? Sometimes I watch the clouds through our classroom window. And when they are white and fluffy I think I see you flying there.

You used to look so beautiful flying low across the paddy field. You couldn't fly very fast, you funny old duck. Remember how I used to chase you and you would squawk and squawk and pretend you were cross with me?

But you always let me catch you, and then I would squeeze you tight and stroke your soft feathers and talk to you. You liked that, didn't you?

Remember the day I chased you right to the edge of the forest?

20

"Don't go in there!" I screamed. "Come back!" But you just squawked and disappeared in the trees. It's really spooky in that forest. Everyone knows there are ghosts there. The trees grow up to the sky and even the sun's little gold arrows can't find their way through the branches.

I crept in very slowly because I didn't want to frighten you. Then I heard something.

"Little duck," I whispered. "Little duck!"

There was a mad scuffling and squawking. Something moved. A black shape. It danced around and waved its arms. It was Grandpa.

"Hello, Grandpa!" I called.

"Sh! Sh!" he said. Then he grabbed you and stuck you in his bag. "Sh! Sh!" he whispered. "We mustn't make a noise. There are soldiers in the forest. They mustn't find us here."

It was very spooky creeping back. It wasn't just the ghosts that were scary—it was the soldiers that might be hiding behind the trees, watching us.

And I wondered what my grandpa had been doing there, all by himself in that black, black forest.

Where are you now, dear little duck? I miss you.

Nam-Huong

Today Mary brought her baby mouse to school, and Miss Lily showed us how to feed it with an eyedropper.

"Come on, my little baby," she said. "Miss Lily won't hurt you. Be a good little mouse and eat up all your lunch. Then you can sleep while we have reading."

Everyone giggled and I heard Danny whisper, "Miss Lily's crazy. She talks to mice!"

But I like her.

Miss Lily is like my dad. He talks to animals, too.

We had drawing at school today. I drew a picture of our house and my dad and his buffalo plowing the field. And then I wrote a letter on the back page of my spelling book.

Dear Mr. Buffalo,

I think of you when Chu Minh sings while he's working in the kitchen. He sounds like you snorting.

Remember how my dad used to talk to you while you pulled the plow around the field or carried a load of rice to the market?

My dad talked to all the animals—but you were his friend. He liked you best.

I wonder where my dad is.

Have you seen him anywhere?

The rice will be ready for picking now.

I wish I were there.

Snort! Snort! my friend Mr. Buffalo.

Nam-Huong

After school today everyone went to the beach. They rode their bikes through the trees at the back of Miss Lily's house.

"Want to come, Nam?" Mary said. "I'll give you a ride. Come on."

But I didn't go.

I don't ever want to go near the sea again.

I don't want to see the sun burning on the water, or the giant waves with white, ugly teeth.

Chu Minh ran out of garlic again today.

"Nam-Huong," he said, and went down on his knees in front of me like he always does when he wants me to help him. "Please, please, my dear little, sweet little, dearest little Nam-Huong, gentle little fragrant breeze of the south, delicate as apricot blossom in springtime—please go quickly to the shop and buy me some garlic as fragrant as a rhinoceros, so that I can finish preparing the soup before your auntie comes back and screams at me like a cross crayfish."

On the way to the shop I passed Miss Lily's house.

I wanted to look in. I wanted to see it. Just for a minute.

So I opened the gate—just a bit. I saw Miss Lily's garden.

It was like a little jungle of ferns and flowers. The little palm tree didn't look like a witch at all.

So I crept in. I put my arms around its rough trunk.

I liked being there. I liked Miss Lily's garden.

But then I saw a black shadow move behind the front window. "Ghosts!" I thought, and I ran away.

When I got back from school today I heard loud music screaming out of the kitchen door. It was so loud and crackly that I had to put my fingers in my ears to stop them from bursting.

"I found it at the dump," Chu Minh said. "It's very old, but now that I've fixed it, it's perfect."

MULCAHEY SCHOOL LIBRARY
TAUNTON, MA 02780

Chu Minh's radio makes him very happy.

But it makes Auntie really mad. She stamps her feet and shouts, "Turn it off!" But Chu Minh doesn't hear. And when she yells out, "Chu Minh, the sauce needs more chili," it makes her even madder when he doesn't answer and just keeps singing along with the music on his radio.

Yesterday Auntie got the big brass bell with the dragon on it from the counter in the restaurant and rang it right in Chu Minh's ear.

"Turn it off now!" she shouted. "How can you make beautiful food in all that noise?" But as soon as she went out shopping, Chu Minh turned it on again.

"The music makes my heart blossom," he said. "It turns my blood into swirling rivers and waterfalls—and only then can I make soups and dishes as fragrant and delicate as jasmine petals."

So I kept guard at the back door and I rang the dragon bell to warn Chu Minh when Auntie was coming. Then he turned off the radio and started scaling the fish and singing.

Auntie came in smiling and said, "That's beautiful, Chu Minh—that's my favorite song."

I walk past Miss Lily's house every day now.
  I like going that way.

"Come and taste this soup for me!" Chu Minh called as soon as I came in this afternoon. "It's wonderful, it's heaven, and I, Chu Minh, have made it for you, my little cloud, my little breeze, and for anyone else who cares to dine tonight at Mrs. Tran's distinguished restaurant, known all over the world from the East to the West for food to delight the palates of emperors and princesses."

I nearly choked when I tasted it. Chu Minh had put so much chili in it that dragon flames leaped right down my throat and I thought the fire in there would never go out.

Chu Minh laughed and laughed and he gave me water to put out the fire and wiped my eyes with his T-shirt and said, "Good, good—the soup is just right—it's *perfect*."

*　　*　　*

"Look what I found at the dump today," Chu Minh said when I came in after school. "It's for you, my little breeze."

It was leaning against the wall outside the kitchen door. When I saw that old bike I thought of Mary's silver bike, and Danny's bike with ten gears, and Tessa's skinny tires. "They're real racing tires," she told everyone.

But I don't mind. As soon as I saw it I liked that bike of mine with its fat tires and its handlebars like buffalo horns.

Every day after school Chu Minh watches me through the kitchen window while I practice riding 'round and 'round our little concrete yard.

One day I'll ride my bike to school.

Miss Lily's back gate was open today so I looked in. There were trees everywhere—trees full of plums.

I saw something moving in the branches. A big straw hat was flopping among the leaves.

It was Miss Lily. Miss Lily was in the tree!

Miss Lily had climbed up a plum tree!

"Hello, Nam," she said. "Come and help me pick some plums."

But a dog was there. He jumped on me and licked me.

"Samson won't hurt," Miss Lily called. "He just wants to be friends."

I climbed up into the tree. I climbed everywhere.

I liked sitting in the leaves.

I liked being there with Miss Lily.

We filled Miss Lily's bucket to the top.

"I'll make plum jam," she said.

Today Miss Lily gave me a jar of her plum jam.

"It's for your auntie," she said.

On the label she had written Miss Lily's Plum Jam.

Auntie was very pleased. So was Chu Minh.

He mixed it up with saté and coconut milk and made a new sauce for the chicken.

We all liked it.

Miss Lily was away sick today.

"I don't reckon she's sick at all," Danny said. "I reckon the ghosts have locked her in a cupboard."

"No, they haven't. The witch has turned her into a spider and she's stuck in a web," Mary said.

Then Tessa shouted, "Hey! What if the witch has made her grow so tall that she can't get out the door?"

I kept thinking about Miss Lily all day— wishing she were here. I don't want her to be sick.

That night I wrote another letter.

Dear little yellow canary,

Do you remember the day we said good-bye?
My mom woke me very early.

"There is a war on in our country," she said, "and
there is fighting everywhere. It's not safe to stay here
in our village. Everyone is leaving—and we must go,
too. I will take the other children to Uncle's house and
wait there for your father. But I want you to go with
Grandpa. You are the oldest, and you can look after
him—and one day soon we will all be together again.
You must leave now. Grandpa knows a man who has
a boat."

When my mom put her arms around me and held
me close to her I wanted to stay there forever.

I couldn't take anything with me, little canary—
only the clothes I was wearing.

And when I opened the door of your cage, I whis-
pered, "Good-bye, my best friend in all the world,"
and I watched you fly away above the trees like a lonely
leaf blown by the wind.

32

Where are you now, little canary?
Have you seen my mom and dad?

Nam-Huong

Today Tessa passed this note around the class and I saw it.

Check the square   YES   NO

Nam-Huong means:
  Potato chips   ☐   ☐
  Dim sim   ☐   ☐
  Meat pie   ☐   ☐
  Froot Loops   ☐   ☐

Tessa climbed onto the roof of our classroom this morning so that she could see the swallows' nest.

She said there were four eggs in there.

Dear little swallows, I thought. How long will it be until you fly back over the sea again? I wish I were a bird—then I would go with you.

33

*   *   *

Something beautiful has happened to my bike.

Chu Minh and I have painted it.

We painted a butterfly on the fender and a little dragon on the handlebars. I put my name on it, too.

"Now it's perfect for my little breeze," Chu Minh said.

Miss Lily was away again today.

That's three days now that she's been gone.

Last night I lay in bed waiting for the morning to come.

Then I would ride my bike to school. I would take it to the bike rack and leave it there with all the other bikes. I would think of it all day, waiting for school to finish so that I could ride out of the school gate with Mary and Tessa and Danny and everyone.

I was still waiting for the morning when the rain started. It knocked loudly on my window.

My bike! I thought.

The rooms were black and still, and ghosts

were everywhere waiting for me in the corners as I crept down the stairs. They were waiting in the kitchen, too, hiding under the table and in the cupboards. I unlocked the door and ran to my bike. How glad I was to see it again.

I wheeled it into the kitchen. Then I stopped. I was sure I heard a ghost in Auntie's saucepan cupboard. But I kept going. If Auntie came down she'd be mad at me.

Past all those spooky ghosts I pushed that beautiful bike. I pulled it slowly up the stairs. I pushed it into my room.

I dried it with my towel and stood it at the end of my bed. I lay and watched it all the night and waited for the day.

The sun was shining in the morning.

Thank you, sun, I thought. I know you are shining for me. You have told the rain to go away so that I can ride my bike to school.

While Auntie was in the bathroom I took my bike downstairs and went outside.

How wonderful it was riding to school. My bike was as beautiful as a poem—that's how much I liked it.

We flew along like birds—my bike and me—and I wished that my mom and dad and Lan and my little brothers and all my friends could see us and wave to us as we went by.

We flew through the gate into the school yard.

"Gee, where'd you get that old heap?" Danny shouted.

Everyone laughed, and I heard Tessa say, "Looks like she found it at the dump."

And someone threw a big lump of mud at

it—and Tessa threw a whole lot of cherry pits.

Then Mary came over and said, "Come on, Nam, I'll help you put it in the bike rack."

I thought about my bike all day.

After school I ran to the bike rack. There were lots of kids standing around—all watching me.

Someone had made my tires go flat. Someone had let the air fly out.

So I wheeled my bike to the gate and along the street.

"Why isn't she cross?" someone said.

"Why doesn't she say something?"

"She's too dumb," I heard them say.

I wished I could tell them how I felt.

I wished I weren't all locked up inside.

I wished I could tell them what wild typhoons had blown away my beautiful day.

When Chu Minh fixed my tires for me he said, "Life is like a fleet-footed horse passing by a crevice. Our families and friends are gone, but you and I are lucky to be safe here in our new land. So, little breeze, little cloud, we mustn't

37

let a handful of mud or cherry pits spoil our day."

And he took one of Auntie's very best glasses that she uses when Mr. and Mrs. Ngoc come over and he balanced it on his nose.

I'm glad Chu Minh lives at Auntie's place. I'm glad she's looking after him, too. He is as skinny as bamboo, but he's as strong as a buffalo.

On Sunday afternoon I went to the park with Auntie and Mr. and Mrs. Ngoc and their children. I rode my bike. I rode it everywhere.

I pretended I was in the city with my uncle and Lan, riding in a trishaw along the busy streets—past the flower market and the bird market selling parrots and monkeys and squirrels, past the big-eyed fish staring at us from the stalls. Faster and faster we went—there were bikes and trishaws everywhere—and I held Lan very tight so that she didn't fall out.

"Nam-Huong!" I heard Auntie calling me. But I didn't want to hear—I wanted to stay on my bike forever.

Dear little duck as white as a cloud,

I'm writing this in my math book. My teacher, Miss Lily, is away sick and the problems that Mr. Brown has given us are too hard.

I wish we were playing together now. I wish I were chasing you across the paddy field.

Dear little duck, it's so long now since I said goodbye to you and walked through the forest with Grandpa. He carried baskets of rice—just as if he were going to the market.

Grandpa and I walked all day, and at night we lay on the ground, and the sounds of frogs and crickets and creatures of the night drowned our dreams.

And I thought I heard a tiger, but I couldn't tell Grandpa, because tigers have very sharp ears and if you say their name they'll hear you and get you.

So I whispered, "Ong Ba Muoi!—Ong Ba Muoi!" instead and Grandpa understood and he held my hand very tight.

Then he opened his basket and gave me some rice

cake and dried fish that my mom had given us to eat on our journey.

And we watched for soldiers. We watched and listened for soldiers all day and all night.

One day the forest came to an end.

I pushed Grandpa up a hill—and there below us we saw the sea.

That's when Grandpa met the man who owned the boat.

Dear little duck—I miss you.

Nam-Huong

"I've made your favorite *cha gio*," Chu Minh said to me after school today. "I made some extra just for you. Here, take them up to your room and eat them there before Auntie comes back—she's been to the doctor and she'll be back soon with her aching head and her knees and her ankles."

Chu Minh gave me the *cha gio* in a bowl. But I didn't eat them.

I ran to Miss Lily's. I opened the gate and tiptoed onto the front veranda. Black corners and cobwebs were there. Ghosts! Suddenly the

41

door opened and a fat man said, "Coming in to see Miss Lily? I'll be on my way now. We've just had a cup of tea. Go in and see her, love—she needs a bit of cheering up."

Miss Lily's hair was flying all over the pillow. Her face was white like her sheets.

And Samson was curled up asleep on her bed. He was snoring there on an old rug made of bits of red and green material.

When I sat on the bed with Miss Lily, Samson woke up and jumped all over me and knocked me over.

"Does my little Samson want his afternoon tea?" Miss Lily said, and she pointed to a big glass jar on her dressing table. It was full of chocolates and jujubes and jelly beans.

"Come on, my little darling," she said, "Nam will give Samson boy his afternoon treat."

Samson dribbled the chocolate I gave him all over his rug and all over Miss Lily's sheet. But she didn't mind.

And she didn't mind when Samson grabbed

one of Chu Minh's special *cha gio* from the bowl. He ate every bit, and Miss Lily smiled and said, "They look delicious. Samson thinks they are, too. We'll have them for our dinner tonight."

I took Miss Lily some soup today.

"Thank you, Nam. It looks beautiful," she said. "Shall we ask Mr. Newton to come in and have some with us? He's all by himself now since his wife died, and I sometimes take him a bit of soup or custard."

Miss Lily wrote a note to Mr. Newton and I went next door and gave it to the man who was watering the garden.

It was the fat man.

"Where are you from?" he asked.

And when I didn't answer he said, "Cat got your tongue, has it?"

Mr. Newton and I sat next to Miss Lily and we all had soup.

Samson had some, too.

Miss Lily didn't have much soup, but Mr.

Newton dunked four slices of bread in his and ate it all—except for the bit he slopped down the front of his T-shirt.

"Not bad," he said when he'd finished. "Not bad. But I don't really go for that sort of fancy stuff. I still reckon you can't beat a can of good old tomato soup, can you?"

I like tidying Miss Lily's room for her and dusting the big old dressing table.

It's covered with all sorts of dangly earrings—there are some with flowers and silver balls and some with cats and lions, and one with a big red jewel and one with an orange fish. The red parrot ones are there, too. I like them best.

Today I saw the bottle of perfume with the flowers on it. I picked it up and looked at the picture.

"Put some on," Miss Lily said.

I rubbed the perfume all over my face and hands and arms and in my hair. It smelled so beautiful and I made Miss Lily's room smell just like my uncle's garden.

"My little Samson wants some, too," she said.

So I put some on Samson's ears, and I danced around in Miss Lily's perfume garden.

But she didn't see me, because she had gone to sleep. She didn't see me smile either.

Auntie bought some flowers at the market this morning.

"They're for Miss Lily," she said.

I took them to Miss Lily's after school.

"Thank you, Nam. I love them," she said.

So did Samson. He ate two carnations.

"As soon as I'm better," Miss Lily said today, "I'm going camping with Mary and Tessa and Danny. In the evening we'll light a campfire and sit around it and watch the flames. And when the sky is sprinkled with thousands of stars and we hear wind whispers in the forest, we'll tell ghost stories—really spooky ones.

"I love ghosts, don't you? Ghosts that can walk through walls and windows, and slam doors at midnight. I've got lots of ghost books with really scary stories in them. It'll be lots of fun—would you like to come?"

Miss Lily went to sleep then, so she didn't see me nod my head.

*   *   *

After lunch on Sunday, Auntie put some chrysanthemums in water in a big pot on the stove. She cooked it and stirred it for hours.

"It's for Miss Lily," she said, and poured it into a jar. "I always take it for my headaches and sore feet. It fixes everything. It'll fix Miss Lily up, too."

Sometimes I love Auntie.

Chu Minh made some *dim sims* for Miss Lily and he wrote her a letter:

> *My heart overflows with wishes for you.*
> *May you soon be well.*

But when I got to Miss Lily's house and opened the gate something was different.

The front blinds were down. I tiptoed round the back.

Samson yelped and barked when he saw me. He was tied up to the outside faucet with a long piece of rope.

"He's been waiting for you all day," old Mr. Newton said over the fence. "Miss Lily's gone to the hospital. The doctor reckons she's got

47

to have some tests done. Them doctors are all the same. They can't stop jabbing in their needles and cutting bits out of you. Twice I've been in for tests myself.

"One time they found something or other that shouldn't have been there—and do you know what?—just as the nurse had given me this lovely custard stuff for my dinner, this silly young doctor comes in with it in a bottle. He thought I'd like to have a look at it, he said. Well, I told him what he could do with it and not to come spoiling my dinner again with bits of my body chopped up in bottles. Anyway, Miss Lily will make sure they don't go cutting her up and sticking her in a bottle, don't you worry. She said she'd be real glad if you'd look after Samson for her—give him his dinner and take him for a walk."

I nodded, and undid Samson's rope and cuddled him. He barked happily, but inside me there were tears—hundreds of them—crying for Miss Lily.

Dear little yellow canary,

My teacher, Miss Lily, is sick and I'm looking after her dog Samson. I took him for a walk after school today.

But I had to run because he pulled his leash so hard—and he couldn't go straight either, so his leash got all tangled up in my legs.

"Hello Samson," everyone said, and they smiled at Samson and me. Even the butcher is Samson's friend—he gave him a bone to take home.

"Miss Lily always brings Samson for his bone on Wednesdays," the butcher said.

Dear little yellow canary, I like Samson, but you are still my best friend in all the world.

Have you seen my mom and dad anywhere?

Nam-Huong

After school today Samson and I went for a walk to the shops. I saw Danny when we walked past the candy store. He gave Samson

a black jelly bean, but Samson spat it out and
then he jumped all over Danny and licked his
face.

Samson and I like walking together.

Dear little yellow canary,

Samson and I played in Miss Lily's garden today.

I wriggled across the grass like a four-legged snake, but Samson looked very scared when I did that and went and hid in the ferns. So I changed into a fierce beast. He liked that much better, and when I chased him 'round and 'round the palm tree he wagged his tail and yelped and barked.

I chased him 'round and 'round seventeen times. Then he had a nap.

That's when I climbed Miss Lily's little palm tree. I climbed right to the top.

When I was halfway up, I looked down and I wished Lan were sitting there on the grass.

But when I reached the top there weren't any co-conuts. Just all those spiky fronds billowing out like a wild witch's hair.

And I saw the sea.

There was sea everywhere. Everywhere I looked.

And where the sea ended and the sky began, I thought I saw a boat. . . .

. . . It was just a little boat with hundreds of people in it with scared eyes, and sad eyes, and eyes drowned in tears—and Grandpa and me. Grandpa was squashed up close to me and he held my hand and put his arm around me when the waves leaped at us across the deck like snarling tigers.

Sometimes, when we were too wet and cold to sleep, Grandpa told me stories for hours and hours until his voice got lost in the wind and the waves.

Every day there was less and less rice for us to eat. But Grandpa always said he wasn't hungry, and he made me eat his share of rice—his little handful.

And when there was no rice or water left, Grandpa and I clung tightly to each other—and we drifted and dreamed through suns as orange as saffron and nights that wrapped around us like black monsters.

Our little boat floated for days and weeks like a leaf on the edge of the world, and I dreamed of a wave as high as a mountain.

Grandpa and I were standing together on top of it, and we waved to all the world as it carried us to the shores of a beautiful land.

But when, one day, I opened my eyes, there was only the sea screaming around us.

And Grandpa's hand was limp in mine.

I wandered in and out of dreams until one night we reached an island.

Nobody cheered or shouted. Nobody sang. We followed each other, silently, like shadows, and dragged ourselves to the shore. The beach was flooded with wailing and tears then. But not mine. My eyes were dry like a desert.

I fell on the beach and thumped my hands angrily on the hard sand, and somewhere deep inside me I screamed, "Grandpa! Grandpa! Mom . . . Dad . . . Grandpa!" And all my tears were locked away inside me—locked away in a secret place. . . .

Dear little yellow canary, I miss you.

Have you seen my mom and dad?

Nam-Huong

"Miss Lily will be coming home today," Mr. Newton said on Saturday. Samson was very excited, and I was, too. Samson was so excited that he didn't know which way he wanted to go when I took him for a walk. He didn't want to come with me. He wanted to go the other way. So he did. He ran away. He ran into the trees. He ran into the trees that go down to the sea.

I ran along the little track. I ran farther and farther into the bushes, but I couldn't see Samson. I ran and ran—and suddenly the bushes ended and there was the wild, screaming sea.

And for a moment I was on the boat again, and the water was gold around the silent bodies I saw floating there—floating on the saffron sea, staring at the saffron sun—and I saw my Grandpa there, silently floating away.

"ONG NOI! ONG NOI!" I screamed. "GRANDPA! GRANDPA!"

And all the world was crying—even the wind and the waves and the gulls that circled above him.

"Please, gulls," I cried, *"look after my dear grandpa on his lonely journey."*

I ran up and down the beach, but I couldn't see Samson's tail wagging anywhere.

"Samson! Samson!" I shouted, and my voice flew around the sky with the wind. Then I saw him—his head bobbing up and down in the waves.

I felt the water like ice around me as I raced

into the sea. I grabbed hold of him and a huge wave lifted us up. It twirled us and tossed us to the bottom of the sea. And I thought we would stay there forever. But another wave came and threw us onto the sand like bits of seaweed.

Then I beat my hands on the sand and the beach was flooded with my tears. I cried for Grandpa and for my mom and dad and Lan and Tri and Son and Tho.

And I cried for my little yellow canary.

My tears poured out like monsoon rains.

That's when someone put their arms around me. "It's me, Nam," Miss Lily said.

I cried and cried again—real tears—and I shouted, "Grandpa! Grandpa!"

And my words poured out from their secret place.

Miss Lily sat and listened while I told her everything. I told her about my mom and dad.

And then I told her about Grandpa.

I told her about the boat.

I told Miss Lily everything—about the refugee camp, and digging wells for water, and being hungry, and wanting my mom, and wanting to die, and waiting and waiting, and dreaming of somewhere to go. . . .

I talked and talked, and my voice cried and danced above us in the sky with the sea gulls.

Miss Lily held me very tight and then she and Samson took me home.

Danny brought a kite to school today.

It twirled and danced high in the wind. But it got stuck in the tree—right at the top of Phantom House.

"I'll get it!" I yelled.

"Look at Nam," everyone shouted as I climbed up.

"I bet she can't get it," Danny yelled.

When I reached Phantom House I took off my shoes.

"Nam-Huong, you come down right this minute," I heard Mr. Brown shout.

But I kept going.

I liked climbing up that tree.

I liked being in that forest of leaves. Like a bird. Like my yellow canary.

When I reached the top I pulled the kite and threw it out of the tree.

"She's got it!" everyone shouted.

Dear little yellow canary, I wish you were up here with me, singing.

"Want to come over to my place?" Mary said to me after school today. "Danny and Tessa are coming over—we're going to paint our bikes."

Tessa and Mary painted their bikes orange and red, and I painted butterflies on their fenders.

But Danny didn't paint his. He stuck hundreds of stickers everywhere—there were football stickers and pop stars and ones with funny faces and "Yes, I am a Movie Star" on them.

And then he asked me to paint a huge green dragon right across the handlebars.

While I was painting, Tessa said, "Tell us what your name means now?"

I smiled and shook my head.

But when we rode up to the shops, I whispered to Mary, "It means 'fragrant breeze of the south.' "

"I like that," she said. "It's beautiful."

On Saturday Miss Lily had lunch at our restaurant. So did Mary and Danny and Tessa and nearly all our class.

Mr. Newton came, too.

Auntie put her best lace cloth and her blue-and-white cups on Miss Lily's table.

I helped serve everyone.

"I hope you like it," I said as I passed around the soup. "It's my dad's favorite. It's called *pho*. My dad says that my mom makes the best *pho* in the world."

Danny liked the dessert best—he had two helpings of stewed banana and sago in coconut milk.

Mr. Newton didn't talk much. He was too busy dunking bread in his soup and trying to use his chopsticks. When he finished, he went and looked in the kitchen. He talked with

Auntie and Chu Minh and they stood at the door and laughed and waved good-bye to him when at last he left carrying bags full of food.

He winked at me and said, "This stuff beats tomato soup any day." And I heard him say to Miss Lily, "What about you and I come and have lunch here next Saturday?"

Miss Lily said, "Thank you. That would be nice another time, but next weekend I'm going camping with Nam and Mary and Tessa and Danny."

Auntie gave me *dim sims* for lunch today.

"Swap you a cake for one of them?" Danny said.

So I did.

Last weekend we went camping with Miss Lily.

I liked it there.

Samson and I had lots of fun swimming in the river, and I found some wood and made a duck for Miss Lily. I carved it the way Grandpa carved one for me so long ago.

I found some yellow flowers, too—just like

the ones in my uncle's garden. I put them on the river and watched them float away.

In the evening we all sat around the camp-fire.

Miss Lily told the scariest ghost stories, and I crept up behind Tessa and poked her, and she screamed and everyone thought it was a ghost.

And they all grabbed me and tickled me, and I laughed and laughed until the tears ran down all over my face like drops of dew.

This morning, while Miss Lily was correcting homework, I saw something move outside our classroom window.

"The swallows are leaving!" I called out, and everyone jumped up and ran to the window.

"They're flying north to look for summer," Miss Lily said.

We watched them swoop and circle in the sky, fluttering and disappearing like leaves in the wind.

"Swallows," I whispered, "please fly over my country. Tell my mom and dad and Lan and

Tri and Son and Tho that I am waiting for them here. Tell them that I love them. Tell them that I will love them forever and wait for them always."